River of Ice

by Linda Baxter

COVER-TO-COVER BOOKS

Perfection Learning®

Cover and inside illustration: Sue F. Cornelison

For Victor Lazare, the real Sasha

About the Author

Linda Baxter was born in Cheyenne, Wyoming, and traveled with her military family, finally settling in Tempe, Arizona. She graduated with a degree in elementary education from Arizona State University. Ms. Baxter taught elementary grades in Phoenix, Arizona, and Catshill, Bromsgrove, England.

She lives with her husband, Dave, and three children in Monte Sereno, California.

For information, contact
Perfection Learning® Corporation
1000 North Second Avenue, P.O. Box 500
Logan, Iowa 51546-0500.
Phone: 1-800-831-4190
Fax: 1-712-644-2392
Paperback ISBN 0-7891-5392-0
Cover Craft® ISBN 0-7807-9805-8
Printed in the U.S.A

Contents

1

The Letter

Sasha pressed his nose to the freezing window. He looked out over the snow-covered square. He was searching for his mother's figure in the winter darkness. He clutched a small blue envelope.

"This has to be the one," he whispered to himself. The envelope crackled in his fingers. "It just has to be the one."

Doctor Marie Bausch walked home from the hospital each evening. Heavy furs kept out the Moscow cold. Tonight she was late. Sasha had waited for his mother for more than an hour.

The intricate icy pattern formed every night on their apartment windows. Tonight it crept toward the center. Soon he would have to scratch through the frost design to see out into the snowy darkness.

"Come back to the fire, Sasha," coaxed Poppy. "Standing there won't get your mama home any faster. You must be freezing by the window."

Sasha reluctantly plopped into the old red chair by the fire. Poppy returned to her darning. Sasha looked anxiously at his nanny.

"Why is she so late tonight, Poppy?" asked Sasha. "I want to open the letter from Da. I know this will be the one. It's so hard to wait."

"I know," said Poppy. She did not even look up from her work. "You know our Madame Doctor. She must take care of everyone who needs her. Perhaps there was an accident or more trouble in the streets. She will be along."

Sasha was unable to sit still, even with the pleasant

heat of the fire. He wandered back to the window. The frost masterpiece glittered in the streetlight. Tonight it reminded him of a tree branching to the sky. With his fingernail, Sasha scratched a small viewing hole in the ice. He spied his mother coming across the square.

"She's home, Poppy!" he shouted. Sasha darted for the door to the hall.

"Wait on the landing," called Poppy. Sasha had already slammed the door behind him.

Sasha dashed to the top of the stairs. He waited impatiently for Mama in the dark hall. Only a street lamp lit the glass in the front door below. Mama's key wiggled in the lock.

Sasha heard a quiet click behind him. He turned to see a strange face staring at him. He gasped in surprise. Then he heard his mother's footsteps on the wooden stairs.

"Sasha, is that you?" Mama called. She squinted through the gloom.

"Yes, Mama," he turned to answer. He looked over his shoulder. The neighbor's door closed silently.

"You are so late, Mama. I was worried. Was there more trouble?" Sasha asked.

The stranger at the door was forgotten.

Mama bustled through the door to their apartment. Sasha trailed behind. The snowflakes sprinkled on her head and shoulders began to melt. She untied her scarf and took off her big fur hat. Poppy helped Mama. It took many layers of clothing to keep out the Moscow winter.

"There was an accident," Mama explained breathlessly to Sasha and Poppy. She smoothed her dark hair back into its confining twist. "A child had been caught under a cart. I didn't dare leave him until I knew he would survive."

"Will he be all right, Mama?" asked Sasha.

Finally unwrapped, Mama hugged Sasha tightly. Sasha let her. Although he felt too old for hugs, he knew they were important to his mama—especially since Da had gone away.

Mama whispered into his ear, "One for now and one for later. I don't know what I would do if I couldn't come home to one of these every night," she said.

Finally she released him. Mama smiled. "And yes, the boy will be fine. He has a bump on the head and a broken arm. He's just about your age."

"Mama, we got a letter from Da and Raisa today. I waited for you to open it. Do you think this is the one? I just know it is. Can we open it now?" asked Sasha excitedly.

Poppy suggested, "Let me get your mama a cup of

hot tea, Sasha. Then you can read it by the fire."

"Oh, yes, please, Poppy," sighed Mama. "Thank you. A coal fire tonight? Where on earth did you find coal? There hasn't been any for months," Mama exclaimed. She warmed her hands near the red glow.

"I waited in a long line," agreed Poppy. "I know where to find most things these days—if they can be found."

"Come here, Sasha," said Mama. "We will read the letter together. Let me get my 'old-lady' glasses. Then I can see the words. You know your da always writes with such small print."

"You're not an old lady, Mama! You just have old-lady eyes," laughed Sasha.

Mama collapsed into the big red velvet chair. Its arms were shiny from years of wear. Sasha sat on the arm of the chair. He felt the warmth of happiness and hope.

"Ah, Sasha," sighed Mama. "I remember when we both fit in this chair. You better stop growing. You will soon be taller than I am."

Sasha smiled at the old joke they always shared. "Yes, Mama. I'm trying to stop. But I can't help it. Poppy said I grew another inch this month! Didn't you, Poppy?"

"Yes, dear," responded Poppy. She handed Mama a

steaming cup of tea. Then the old woman took a small chair opposite them.

Mama huffed, but smiled. She smoothed Sasha's soft curls away from his face. Then she looked deep into his brown eyes.

"You will be tall, just like your father. You look just like him—even at 12."

"Here is the letter, Mama." Sasha took the square envelope from the table. He handed it to her. It made a small crackly sound as she undid the seal. She pulled out the thin sheets of pale blue paper.

Da and Sasha's sister, Raisa, had been gone a very long time. Sometimes it was hard for Sasha to remember his father and older sister. So he would look at the picture on the mantle. He would study the four of them sitting by the river. Then the memories would flood back.

Mama sighed and began to read.

Riga, Latvia
February 1934

To my darling Marie and my son
Sasha,

The winter has seemed long this year.
Then just last week, the ice began to
break up. Spring cannot be far now. I
know that you will need to wait a bit
there in Moscow. Do not give up hope. I
will think of you as the larks return.

Raisa sends her love. She will soon be
graduating from school. Then she will
join me at the business. I know she will
be a great help.

The factory where I work is doing
well. My health has been much better
this winter. The weather is not nearly
as cold here as in Moscow. I have been
able to continue working every day. You
know what an improvement that is.

Sasha, how is school? Do you like it this year? How is your friend Albert Ivanovich? Have you gone skating on the river this winter? How is Poppy? I know you mind her and Mama the best you can.

*Take care of each other and trust in God (even though **Lenin** says you can't).*

Your Husband and Da,
Victor Petrovich Bausch

Poppy sputtered. "You better put that letter in the fire right now," she said. "What if the wrong person finds that? We could all be sent to **Siberia** or worse."

Mama sighed. "Victor just won't accept the way things are now."

"Mama, can I keep just the first page?" urged Sasha "You could just burn this part about Lenin."

"Yes, that would work. Here, Sasha, go put this with the others," agreed Mama.

Sasha took the first page of the letter. He stood on the footstool next to the high carved mantel. The warm fire baked his knees as he placed the page in a wooden box. It joined many other pale blue papers. The letters spanned more than two years.

"Is there a secret note?" asked Sasha.

Mama picked up the envelope. She carefully slit the side. Sasha and Poppy waited silently. Sasha's heart gave a loud thump. Da often hid a small note between the envelope's two thin sheets. Sure enough, a small piece of paper fell out of the envelope. Mama read the tiny print.

Darlings,

We are saving everything we can in the hope that soon you will be able to join us. There has been no change in news from Germany. I am afraid the money invested before the war is lost to us.

*With the government as it is, Raisa and I cannot risk coming back. **Stalin** does not trust those on the outside now. We would all be sent to Siberia.*

Has there been any progress? We heard rumors that Stalin has allowed a few families to emigrate. I urge you to try again. There is little time. Stalin's grip continues to tighten.

I have heard through friends that Lazare will be released from prison soon. Marie, go to him. He may be able to help. VP

Sasha continued to stare at the letter. He said sadly, "It wasn't the one. They are not coming back. And we cannot go to them."

After a moment, Mama replied, "No."

In the firelight, Sasha noticed the lines that creased her forehead. "Sometimes I wonder if we will ever be together again," sighed Sasha.

"I know, Sasha," consoled Mama. "But we must not give up hope."

"Why does it have to be like this? Why are we always pulled apart?" cried Sasha angrily. "I want to be with everyone."

"One day . . ." started Mama. Then she looked away.

Poppy bustled about, clearing cups. She poked at the fire angrily. A blaze of tiny sparks flew up the chimney.

Mama smiled at the old woman's efforts. "It won't do any good to poke the fire to death," she said.

"But I'll feel better," huffed Poppy. She replaced the poker and sat down.

"Mama, who is Lazare?" Sasha asked.

"Just an old friend of your father's," Mama tried to answer lightly.

She stood. "Now it is time for bed. There is school tomorrow." Sasha knew that she was pretending to be cheerful.

"I'll go get ready. Have something to eat, Mama. Poppy made **borscht** for dinner," Sasha said. "I know that's your favorite soup. And there's sour cream to turn it pink." He tried to smile.

"That's fine," said Mama. "I'll come and check on you in a moment. And, Sasha, never give up hope."

Sasha made his way to the door. Then he turned to

watch. Mama picked up the secret message and read it again. Sasha wondered if perhaps she hoped for a change as much as he did.

She tossed the note into the fire. A bright blue flame consumed the message. Mama walked wearily out of the room.

2
The Man Behind the Door

In the morning, Sasha waited for his friend Albert. Sasha hummed a little tune to himself. They always met on the stairs by Sasha's door. There had been no trouble in the streets this winter. So they were allowed to walk to school together again.

Albert lived upstairs. Sasha could hear his feet thumping down the stairs, two flights up. He hoped Albert would hurry. Their teacher, Madame Vickor, expected them to be on time.

Sasha heard the door behind him open. The hinge squeaked. He turned to see the same strange old man staring out at him. Sasha felt goose bumps creep down the back of his neck. Now he knew he had not imagined the searing eyes in the dark hall.

The man's pale skin was stretched tightly over the bones of his skull. His bright blue eyes bulged from sunken sockets. The stranger said nothing. He just stared at Sasha. The old man's eyes swept up and down. Sasha was afraid to move.

Albert turned the corner of the stairs. He leaped down the last three steps as he swung around the newel post. Sasha glanced at his friend. Then he looked back at the old man.

The door closed. The stranger was gone. Sasha shook off the icy feeling. He joined his friend in a race to the front door.

"Did you see the old man?" Sasha asked Albert. They walked along the city street to the nearby school.

"Not this morning. Did he peek out at you too? I saw him the other day when I was waiting for you," said Albert. "My father says he is Madame Lazaronova's father."

Albert leaned over. He whispered in Sasha's ear. "My father told my mother that the old man just got out of the **gulag**. He said something to the wrong person. So they put him in prison. That's what my father said. My mother said that he really isn't that old. He was just treated very badly in the gulag."

"How do you hear all this, Albert Ivanovich?" asked Sasha.

Albert ran his hand through his bright red curls. His blue eyes flashed. His freckles seemed to glow. He grinned.

"I listened at the door," he boasted. "Sometimes it's the only way to know what's going on. You don't think my parents want me to know those things, do you? "

Sasha shook his head.

"I sneak down the back hall in my bare feet," Albert explained. "I even know which of the floorboards creak. My parents always talk in the kitchen when they think I am asleep. You should try it, Sasha."

Sasha smiled and said, "I know I would get caught."

Albert grinned. But then, Albert grinned all the time. Albert even grinned when he was in trouble at school. He grinned when old Madame Vickor punished him. It always made the teacher so angry when Albert couldn't stop grinning.

The two boys entered the school grounds. A few students stood outside the school in the cold dawn.

Two brave souls were heaping gray snow into a pile.

Sasha and Albert climbed the steep stone steps. They entered the hush of the school hall. There was no talking allowed in the hall. Sasha and Albert winked quickly at each other. Then they entered their classroom.

A clanging bell echoed through the school. The students sat silently in neat rows. No one was allowed to slouch. Sasha tried to concentrate on his Latin grammar. But he kept seeing the searing blue eyes of the old man staring back at him.

Sasha stared out the window at the barren exercise field. Only one window in the classroom had not been painted over.

Madame Vickor stood at the front of the classroom. She droned on about today's Latin lesson. He understood the lesson. So Sasha allowed himself to daydream again.

"Sasha," the teacher called loudly. Her voice echoed in the high-ceilinged room.

Madame Vickor called on him again. He fumbled to stand and recite. Impatiently, his teacher repeated the question in Latin. "Who will help you? *Quis iuvabit te*?"

Sasha stood at attention beside his desk. Without thinking, he replied, "The old man will help me. *Vir senex me iuvabit*."

"That is good," replied Madame Vickor. But she was still frowning. "Next time be ready with your reply."

"Sorry, madam," apologized Sasha.

"Yes," Sasha whispered to himself. He returned to his seat. "Perhaps the old man can help."

Sasha stared out the window.

That evening, Sasha sat by the steps near the old man's door. He hoped the skeleton man would reappear. Poppy had to call him twice before he heard her. The man did not appear.

The following morning, Sasha waited for Albert. He made an extra effort to whistle loudly. The old man still didn't show his face. Then on the third day, Poppy asked him to take a message to that very apartment.

Suddenly, Sasha was not so sure he wanted to see the skeleton man with the piercing blue eyes. He stood at the door for several minutes.

Finally he summoned the courage. He knocked hesitantly. No answer. Sasha knew that Poppy would be angry if he did not deliver the note. He knocked again—this time more firmly.

Muted footsteps shuffled behind the door. Sasha felt his throat go dry and tight. The door locks unbolted. He held his breath. Madame Lazaronova opened the door. She smiled kindly at Sasha.

"Good afternoon, Sasha," she said. "Come in, please. I have to take the **pirog** from the oven or the pastry will overcook. I will be right back."

Sasha felt calmer now. He waited in the darkened hallway. Then he heard raspy breathing. He turned to see the blue-eyed man staring at him.

The man walked slowly toward him. He barely picked up his feet. Carefully, he steadied himself with a cane. His back was bent. His sparse gray hair hung over his eyes. Sasha's feet were frozen to the floor as he stared.

Madame Lazaronova returned to the hall. She said briskly, "Sasha, you don't remember my father, do you? Father, this is **Alexander Victorovich Bausch** from next door. He is Madame Doctor's boy."

Suddenly the piercing blue eyes crinkled into a smile. The rest of the very thin face followed. There were gaps in the smile where teeth should have been. Only then did Sasha take a breath.

The old man extended his bony hand toward Sasha. He said, "It is good to see you again. I know your papa well. How is he doing in Riga?"

Sasha shook the hand offered to him. He replied hesitantly, "He is well, sir." The man's hand felt like bones bundled in dry paper.

The old man continued, "I know you probably don't remember me. You were very young when I . . ." The old man hesitated. " . . . when I went away. I know your father and mother. It is good to see you are growing up into such a fine lad. Do they still call you *Sasha*?"

"Thank you, sir. Yes, my family calls me that," replied Sasha. "I brought a note from Poppy." He handed the paper to the woman.

"Father, you should go and rest now," said Madame Lazaronova gently. "I will have your dinner ready in a while."

"Good-bye, lad," said the old man. He turned and shuffled down the dark hall.

Madame Lazaronova read the note quickly. "Sasha, your mother has invited us to dinner tomorrow evening. We would be pleased to come. Will you tell her that 7:00 is fine? I know it will do my father good to see your mother. Give my love to Poppy."

Madame Lazaronova led Sasha to the door. "Good-bye, Sasha."

Sasha was consumed with curiosity. He rushed back to his apartment. Poppy was ironing in the kitchen. Sasha asked her about the old man.

Poppy frowned and said, "Poor Lazare."

"Why is he so terribly thin?" asked Sasha. "Is he very old? Is he sick?"

Poppy looked stern. She stopped smoothing the old tablecloth with the heavy iron. "So many questions," she said.

"Where has he been?" continued Sasha. "He said he had been away. He said it in a strange way." He thought for a long moment. "Is he the Lazare in Da's letter?"

Sasha watched Poppy's frightened face. With a clang, she set the heavy iron back on the hot stove. She wiped her brow with her apron. Then she put her hands on Sasha's shoulders.

She said, "Sasha, there are things you don't understand. Things in Russia are very difficult. Perhaps you should speak to your mother. She should be home early tonight. If you ask her, I think she will explain."

Poppy turned back to her ironing.

Sasha sighed. "Always I have to wait."

3

Lazare

Sasha, Mama, and Poppy finished dinner that evening. Sasha again asked his question. "What happened to Madame Lazaronova's father?"

A long silence followed. Sasha watched Mama's

face for an answer. Poppy began to pick up the dishes. She left the dining room quickly.

Mama turned to Sasha. She said, "Alexander Victorovich . . . Sasha, you are becoming a fine young man. I have kept many of the problems in Russia from you. I know you have seen the posters about the **Russian Revolution**. Do you remember the nights when there was fighting in the streets? There is much fear now for the people in Russia—much hardship. It is difficult to explain it all."

Sasha waited as Mama took a moment. She searched for the right words. Then she explained, "Lazare Gregorovich was a successful man at one time. He built a fine business. However, he did not agree with the men who headed the government. He foolishly criticized a newly powerful man.

"Lazare has spent the last five years in the gulag. It is a difficult place to survive. Many do not. He was recently released. Now he has come to stay with his daughter. Your father and Lazare used to be very good friends.

"It is important to understand that Lazare is not a bad man. He needs our help to recover from his experience. I know I can trust you not to speak of him to anyone. He is not to be discussed with your friends. It is very important."

Sasha nodded. "Yes, Mama. May I ask Lazare

Gregorovich about my father?"

Mama smiled, "Yes, dear. I'm sure he would love to speak to you about many things."

Poppy shopped in the long rows of the outdoor market. Sasha followed, pulling a small sled.

It was a windy day. The canvas roofs of the traders' tents whipped in the breeze. Tiny snowflakes whirled in the wind.

Poppy bartered for necessities—cabbage, flour, potatoes, salt. She also bought butter and eggs when she could find them.

The butcher had meat today. The animals were hunted in the wild and then frozen in the natural cold. Today, they were lucky. Poppy bought a leg of wild boar.

"Oh, look, Sasha. There is sugar today," exclaimed Poppy. "I think we can afford a bit. Your mama wanted to have a real feast for Lazare and his daughter."

Sasha savored a small chunk. The merchant filled a cloth bag for them.

"I'll hold the eggs and butter for you," said Sasha.

"Okay, but be sure no one takes the cabbages and potatoes," cautioned Poppy.

"I'll keep watch," he assured her. Sasha kept a watchful eye. Poppy scoured the market for bargains.

Then Sasha found apples. They had been preserved over the winter in a cellar. Now they were sold at a steep price. Poppy looked at the few **kopecks** left in her hand.

"We could use four apples if you can get them for two kopecks," she said to Sasha.

"Let me try," said Sasha.

Poppy waited at a distance. Sasha faced the apple seller. He pointed to the best apples.

"I will pay you one kopeck for four of those small apples," he said.

"That is the best of my crop," said the man. He crossed his arms. "I can take no less than four kopecks."

Sasha looked uninterested. He turned to go. "Too high for last year's crop," he said.

The man quickly responded, "All right. How about three good apples for two kopecks?"

"Make it five apples for two kopecks," countered Sasha quickly.

The man smiled and then nodded. Sasha handed over the coins. "A good bargain," said the merchant.

Poppy let Sasha eat the extra apple. They carted home the day's shopping. Sasha looked forward to the evening feast.

When they returned home from the market, Sasha helped Poppy prepare the meal. He helped her chop the cabbage and beets for the borscht. Sasha liked to stir the magenta-colored soup. His mouth watered as it bubbled on the stove.

Albert came to help too. Together they rolled the warm, sweet bread dough into dinner rolls. Sometimes it stuck to their fingers. When Poppy pretended she wasn't looking, the boys stole small nips.

The meat roasted in the oven. The kitchen held wonderful smells. It snowed all afternoon, but Sasha didn't care.

That evening, Sasha was the first to the door as their guests arrived. Again Lazare's blue eyes crinkled into a smile as he greeted Sasha.

"Good evening, sir," said Sasha. "Please come sit by the fire. I am glad you could come, Madame Lazaronova."

The old man moved into the parlor very slowly. His daughter helped him along. With a slow grunt, he settled himself into the large chair. His gnarled hands held his cane in front of him.

Looking around, Lazare caught his breath. He whispered, "Thank you, Sasha. Ah, this room hasn't changed much. I used to play chess here with your father. Do you still have that fine old set?"

Mama entered the room. She responded, "No. Victor

took it with him when he went to Latvia. I knew it would give him pleasure there. It is so good to see you, Lazare."

They kissed the traditional Russian way—three times, back and forth, on the cheek.

"It is good to see you again, Sonia," said Mama to Lazare's daughter. They hugged each other warmly.

Sasha could picture the chess set in his mind. He could remember his father pointing to each delicately carved piece. Da had taught Sasha the moves of the game.

Sasha sat on the stool by the fire. He waited as Mama served wine to the guests. He studied the man's gaunt face secretly.

"Ah, a fine wine," Lazare said to Mama as he took a small sip.

"We managed to save a few bottles," replied Mama. She sat close to Lazare. She took his hand in hers, saying, "How are you, old friend?"

Lazare shrugged his sharply angled shoulders. "I will recover. There is not much they did not try at the gulag. Yet I survived. Food and rest is all I need. And good friends."

"It is good to have you back," said Mama.

Sonia said, "I am still worried about his cough, Marie. Sometimes he cannot catch his breath."

"That will improve with time. Do you need extra

food? Poppy can bring you something each day if you can't manage," offered Mama.

"No, no," laughed Lazare. "My daughter feeds me six times a day as it is. I will be fine. I am already filling in the hollow places." He patted his very lean middle.

Poppy entered the room to show them to dinner. Sasha had not seen a banquet set on their table in a long time. The steaming roast fogged the windows. There were two kinds of smoked fish, fresh cabbage salad, and potatoes. For dessert, they had **blini** and jam. Sasha loved the thin pancakes filled with sweet jam.

As they finished the meal, Lazare said, "Poppy, you have outdone yourself. In the gulag, I dreamed many times of the meals I had enjoyed here. I would pretend I was eating your beautiful dinner rolls, when all I had was moldy bread. I am sure it is the reason I live today."

Poppy blushed. She hurried to clear away the dishes. Sasha saw the tears in her eyes.

"Tell me about my dear friend, your husband, Marie. How is he doing in Latvia?" asked the old man.

Mama replied, "He and Raisa left just over two years ago. Victor had been very ill that winter. He was unable to work for over a year. We convinced the emigration authority that he would not survive. Raisa was allowed to go with him to care for him. They went to Paris first to see a doctor. Then they settled in Latvia.

"They would not let me emigrate," Mama continued. "A doctor is too important to the state to be allowed to leave. As a woman doctor, I am also an example of the 'success of the Revolution.' Sasha was too young to make the trip. So we are still here. I keep trying to convince the authorities that we must leave too." Sasha heard the frustration in her voice.

Sasha had heard about going to Latvia to be with his father many times. He missed his father very much. Yet he could not imagine how could he leave Poppy or Albert behind.

He wished his father would just come back here. But no, then Da might get sick again. Confusion and fear crowded into his mind. He couldn't stay in the room.

"Mama," he said quietly. "May I go see if Albert is home? We don't have school tomorrow."

Mama nodded. "Just for a little while."

"Good-bye," Sasha said to Lazare.

"Come play chess with me sometime, Sasha," called the old man.

"Yes, sir," replied Sasha. "Good night."

Sasha went to his room for a moment to change. He looked back into the parlor on his way out. He heard

Lazare say, "You must keep trying. Things in Russia will not improve. Sasha must find a way out."

"Yes, I know," sighed Mama. She patted his thin hand.

4

Game of Chess

Sasha sat at the kitchen table sipping his tea. He watched Poppy bustle about. The **samovar** sang and hissed a comforting song. Sasha enjoyed the sound of the boiling water. He stirred his clear glass of warm tea with a spoon.

For a moment, Poppy wasn't looking. He quickly popped a brown lump of sugar into his mouth from the sugar bowl. Then he sipped the hot tea through the cube just as he had seen the old men do. The sugar cube dissolved on his tongue. Sasha gave it a final sweet crunch.

Delicious smells drifted from the old oven. They made his mouth water. He loved the apple pirog best of all. Poppy drew the tart from the oven. It was crisp and brown. Precious cinnamon sugar oozed from the edges. She set it on the old table, holding it carefully with her apron.

"Now, Sasha," said Poppy, "This will cool soon. I want you to take it to Madame Lazaronova and her father." She leaned over the steaming pastry and smiled to herself.

"I made it with extra butter and sugar," she explained. "We will get Lazare on the mend. I have some extra soup too."

"He's so thin, Poppy," Sasha said. "I can see all the bones in his face. The gulag must have been something awful."

Poppy sat down across the table. She poured a measure of strong tea for herself. The small teapot perched on top of the samovar. Then she added boiling water from the reservoir.

Frizzled white hair wreathed her face. Wisps

escaped from the braids that crowned her head. The late afternoon light shone through like a halo.

Poppy nodded. Then she said in a serious tone, "It is always unwise to speak before those you do not know and trust. Lazare Gregorovich felt strongly about the freedoms that were hoped for after the revolution. Then those freedoms were denied. He saw the famine coming," she sighed. "But I should let him explain himself."

She sighed, "Go and wash up. Then you can be my messenger."

Sasha stood before the door. He knocked with his foot. His hands were loaded with Poppy's feast.

After a long while, he heard the soft shuffle. The door unlatched. Blue eyes peered out at him. Then the door swung open.

"Daughter, daughter. Come and see what an angel has sent us," called the old man. Madame Lazaronova hurried to the door. She relieved Sasha of his fragrant burden.

"Thank you, Sasha. Oh, Father, Poppy is really spoiling you," she laughed happily.

"Come in and sit down, Alexander Victorovich," wheezed the old man. "Come and sit in the winter sunshine."

Lazare settled himself in his tattered chair. He offered a small wooden stool to Sasha.

"Tell me something, Alexander Victorovich." The old man hesitated. "May I call you Sasha?" He didn't wait for an answer.

"What will you do on this glorious day? You do not have school today? No, of course you don't. School is only six days a week," Lazare said.

"Will you do something with friends?" Lazare asked. "I have seen you with the red-haired lad. Is he a friend?"

"Yes, sir. Albert and I are going ice skating this afternoon. Mama says it may be one of the last days. Soon the ice will break on the river," replied Sasha.

"Ah, a good choice for a clear, cold day. I used to enjoy a good skate on the river," said Lazare. He looked out his window. "Your father and I used to spend many Sundays on the ice."

"Have you known my father a long time?" asked Sasha.

"Your father and I were friends from school," said the old man. "I am a few years older than he. We grew up together. I have been gone for five years. You don't remember me, do you? I held you when you were only days old," the old man sighed.

"My father has been gone for two years. Sometimes I can't remember his face," Sasha said sadly.

"What *do* you remember of your father?" the old man asked.

"Well, there are many little pictures in my mind," Sasha replied. He thought back. "I can remember the times we played chess together. Da taught me to play. He took the chess set with him when he went to Latvia. I remember that Mama insisted."

"Ah, yes, the chess set," said Lazare. He leaned back in his chair. He stared at the graying carved plaster of the ceiling.

"Daughter, can you find my old chess set? I had it in that trunk." The old man struggled to his feet. He grabbed for his cane.

"Don't shout, Father," said Sonia as she returned to the room. "I know where it is. I unpacked those things last week. Sit down, Father. I'll go and get it. Sasha, come with me. You can get up on the chair and reach it."

Sasha followed the woman into the long darkened hall. She reached overhead and opened a high cupboard. Then she moved a chair over.

"Can you see it toward the back? It's a red wooden case." She pointed. Sasha climbed onto the chair. He saw the box and retrieved it.

"Thank you, dear," she said.

Sasha returned to the room. He handed Lazare the red box.

"That's it. Thank you, Sasha," Lazare said.

The old man set the carved pieces on the wooden

playing table. Sasha picked up the white queen. He turned it over in his fingers.

"It's like my father's," whispered Sasha.

"Yes. I have had this set for many years. It was rumored that it once belonged to a prince," the old man whispered to Sasha. Then he winked.

"Your father always admired it. After much searching, I found another one carved in the same style. I presented it as wedding gift when he married your mama."

Lazare placed the white queen in her place of honor. He turned to Sasha and said, "Would you like a game? I will give you my queen. That way it will be more interesting." The old man rubbed his hands together. His eyes twinkled.

Sasha nodded. The two settled their heads over the carved pieces. Sasha wished to impress his new friend. He tried hard to concentrate on the game. He carefully moved his pieces in the attack position his father had taught him.

The old man studied the board. He rubbed the gray stubble on his chin. "A fine beginning, my son. Your father has taught you well."

The old man moved his bishop into position. He said, "Here is the defense."

Sasha groaned. In only a few moves, Sasha knew he had lost.

The old man laughed. "Never mind, boy. Next time I will teach you the counter. Then even I will have a challenge on my hands."

Two games and a win later, Sasha remembered he was expected home for lunch.

5

River of Ice

Sasha and Albert skated until their legs ached. The cold had numbed their noses. They slid into one of the benches that lined the river's edge, stopping to catch their breath. Sasha put his gloved hands over his mouth and nose. He breathed the warm air onto his face. His nose tingled as the blood thawed.

Sasha rubbed his hands together. "Albert, your cheeks are as red as your hair."

Albert laughed. "I don't feel the cold. I think that is the fastest I have ever gone across the river. Papa's skates are great. He says that you can't get good skates like these now."

Sasha agreed. "You can't get any skates now. Poppy and I looked for a new pair. Mine are getting too small. Poppy said she will find me a pair somewhere."

Sasha unlaced his skates. Tying the laces together, he slung the skates over his shoulder.

"Come on, Albert. Let's go get some hot **chai** to drink. The tea will warm us," Sasha promised. "If we run, we can be home and warm in no time."

The boys rushed from the river's edge. Their skates thumped on their shoulders. They quickly climbed the slope to the road above.

They clattered up the apartment stairs. The boys raced to see who could make the landing first. Then they burst into Sasha's apartment. The boys almost knocked Mama over.

"Slow down, slow down! Poppy has the chai on to heat. Take off those wet clothes. Here, come close to the fire. Did you run all the way home?" Mama laughed.

"We're hungry, Mama. We skated up and down the river five times. Albert beat me twice. But I was faster the other two times. There were so many people on the ice. It was wonderful!" exclaimed Sasha.

"I won three times if you count the first lap," corrected Albert. He hung up his hat and scarf.

"You can't count that one, Albert," countered Sasha. "That little girl got in my path. I had to go around."

"Come on, you two. You would think you were competing for the **czar's** jewels," Mama said.

Mama poured the hot chai. "Sasha, I've received a letter from your father's parents," she said. "They have asked you to come for a visit. For the state holiday. Would you like to take the train to see them?"

"Can you come this time too?" asked Sasha. He added sugar to his chai. "I liked going with Poppy last summer. But this time, I want you to come too."

"Yes, I will try. I have not had a holiday in almost two years. It is time," agreed Mama. "We will both go. By then it should be much warmer too."

That evening, Sasha couldn't sleep. The house had been quiet for a long time. He tried to clear his mind. But he saw pictures every time he closed his eyes. He stared into the darkness.

Maybe Albert is right, thought Sasha. Maybe I do need to know more than Mama wants me to know.

Sasha crept out of bed. Carefully, he opened his door. He practiced moving silently up and down the hall. This isn't hard, he thought. He was just beginning to relax.

"What are you doing?" exclaimed Poppy. Sasha jumped. He turned quickly to face his nanny. Sasha tried not to look as guilty as he felt. He wondered how long she had been watching him.

"And what on earth are you doing without your slippers on? You'll freeze," continued Poppy.

"I . . . I was hungry. I didn't want to bother anyone," lied Sasha. His ears warmed.

Poppy crossed her plump arms over an ample middle. Looking skeptical, she said sternly, "Go back to bed."

Sasha hurried down the hall to his small bedroom. He closed his door, moaning softly. How does Albert do it? I should have known I would get caught, he scolded himself.

Sasha turned away from the chess game and glanced out the window. He could see the snow piling up in the center square. He sighed.

"I thought it was almost spring," he said to Lazare. "Now look, it's back to our winter prison."

Lazare squinted out the window. He said, "This is just a temporary setback. This snow will melt quickly as soon as it warms again."

Lazare turned back to study the chessboard. He moved his bishop to challenge Sasha's rook.

Sasha smiled to himself as he closed the trap. He moved his knight to checkmate the black king. Lazare looked up in surprise. The old man laughed. His hands rubbed his crinkled face.

"Sasha, you have improved. Congratulations! It is good to play with a master again."

Sasha smiled. He felt very pleased with himself. "Good game," he said.

"Yes. And that was clever trying to distract me with the weather," laughed Lazare. He shook his finger at Sasha in mock disapproval.

"Yes, distraction is sometimes necessary," the old man said to himself. He looked lost in thought.

"What do you mean?" asked Sasha.

"Oh, never mind, Sasha," replied Lazare.

Sasha began to gather the chess pieces. "May I ask you a question, Lazare? What did you say that caused all the trouble for you?" asked Sasha hesitantly.

For just a moment, Sasha thought that Lazare was angry. Then the old man's weary face relaxed.

"I objected to the division of the wealth in Russia. I disagreed with the plan for the production of food," responded Lazare. He straightened his stooped shoulders.

"I don't understand," said Sasha.

Lazare stared at the chess set placed between them. Then he reached to retrieve the crust of bread remaining from his lunch.

"Set up the white pieces, Sasha," said Lazare. He broke the crust into small pieces.

Sasha quickly returned the chess pieces to their starting positions. Lazare placed a large piece of bread in front of the king and queen. Then he set smaller pieces in front of the bishops, knights, and rooks. The pawns in front had tiny crumbs.

"This is how things were in Russia," explained Lazare. "The czar had the most. The rich had a great deal. And the peasants had little."

Lazare broke the large pieces belonging to the queen and king. He shared the bread more evenly to all the pieces on the board.

"This was the dream of how it would be after the revolution. Everyone would have some. But it was only a dream," continued the old man sadly.

"That seems fair, Lazare," said Sasha. He studied the board. "What went wrong?"

"War took away much of the bread," the old man explained. He scooped more than half of the crumbs away. "And poor administration, greed, stupidity, and fear took more," he said bitterly. He scooped up most of the remaining crumbs.

"Until there is only this," he said as he removed the king, queen, and bishops. Small crumbs remained in front of the rooks and knights. The pawns had nothing.

"What will we do?" asked Sasha, staring at the chessboard.

"Russia will starve," whispered Lazare. "This is what I foretold five years ago to the knights and rooks." He shrugged his thin shoulders. "But they did not want to hear."

The old man carefully swept the remaining crumbs into his hand. He opened the window and spread them on the sill.

"For the larks when they return," he sighed.

6

The Black Queen

"Sasha," Mama said. "I need to speak to you."

Sasha put down the book he had been reading. He looked up at his mother. She sat on the edge of the window seat. Sasha curled his long legs under him.

Outside, the air was still. Snow fell in gentle waves.

It drifted down from low gray clouds.

"You and I need to go see an official at the emigration office tomorrow," said Mama.

"Are we going to try to get **visas** again?" asked Sasha. He felt both hopeful and apprehensive.

"Yes," replied Mama. "I have heard there are some new regulations. Remember, the ones your da wrote about? We need to find out if we can emigrate now."

"I hope this will be the time, Mama," Sasha thought out loud. "Then we can see Da."

Sasha knew that going to emigration meant standing in the cold for hours. Then there would be a long wait on a hard bench while Mama pleaded their case again. He did not mind, he told himself. This might be the time.

"Yes, maybe this time," echoed Mama. She patted him on the knee.

The morning was cold, gray, and overcast. The wind blew handfuls of sleet against his window. Sasha hurried to dress. He grabbed the clothes that Poppy had placed at the foot of his bed. He dressed quickly under the blankets. He shivered as he put on cold socks. Then he buttoned his clean, stiff shirt.

"Poppy," he called out the door. "Shouldn't I wear

my best clothes to the emigration office?"

Poppy had laid out his patched play trousers. And the starched shirt was getting tight.

"No," called Poppy from the kitchen. "Wear what I put out." She was drying her hands on her big apron as she entered his room.

"Your mama said for you to wear clean, *old* clothes. The officials always look at the way you are dressed. If you have nice clothes, they will try to find a way to get more bribes out of you. That's what your mama said."

She turned to go. "Hurry up now, Sasha. You need a big warm breakfast before standing in that cold line. Perhaps you should put on two pairs of socks this morning."

"Well, that would keep my feet warmer. But then my boots feel so tight," replied Sasha.

"Best to have comfortable feet," said Mama as she joined them. "Come, Sasha. We need to be early so you can still get to school for part of the day."

Sasha wrinkled his nose. "I hope it's a long, long line. Then I won't have to do Latin today."

Mama smiled as they walked down the hall and into the warm kitchen. "Mmm," said Sasha. "**Kasha** for breakfast." Sasha enjoyed the steaming hot porridge.

The sleet continued into the morning. Mama and Sasha walked silently through the early morning streets. They stood before an imposing stone building. A thin line of silver dawn struggled to lighten the eastern sky.

The iron gates were still closed. A few brave souls already waited in the pale light. The hopeful stamped their feet to keep warm. Streams of frosty breath floated through the air. People's faces were hidden under layers of tattered clothing. A small child huddled near her mother's long, heavy skirt.

As the day slowly brightened, more people joined the line. It snaked around the building. Soon it disappeared out of sight down the side street.

Sasha kept one hand in his pocket. He buried his nose in his scarf. The sleet crusted the top of his hat with drippy ice. He held his collar tightly around his neck to keep the frigid droplets from sneaking down his back. The feeling in his toes had disappeared an hour ago.

"Shouldn't be too long now," Mama said. "At least we will be allowed to wait inside soon."

A tall guard approached the decorative iron gate. The man was hidden in an oversized gray coat and fur hat. He jangled a huge set of keys in one hand. In the other, he carried a long rifle. He unlocked the gate slowly. The hinges creaked.

"Only the first three," the guard shouted.

Sasha cheered. Then he remembered to be quiet.

The guard glared. With the other hopefuls, Sasha and his mother followed the guard up the dirty steps. They entered the building. It didn't seem much warmer in the echoing hall.

The guard took their names. "Wait here until you are called," he gruffed. He pointed to hard benches outside a set of double doors. They sat.

The guard marched down the hall. His hard, shiny black boots clacked against the marble floor. Turning stiffly, he stood at attention beside the entrance.

Sasha was trying hard to breathe softly. He didn't want anyone to notice him.

"It will be fine, Sasha," Mama whispered into his ear. "No one will hurt us. Just be quiet."

Sasha nodded. He was afraid to speak. All he could think about was Lazare's gaunt face. Would they send his mother to the gulag? Or him? He just wanted to see his father and his sister again.

"Think of something nice," whispered his mama. She rubbed his cold fingers in hers.

Sasha tried to think about his big sister, Raisa. When he was little, they had spent many days playing in the park. And she had taught him to ice skate. She had held his hand until he learned how to glide across the frozen river.

He remembered that Raisa had always tickled him. And she had often shared her sweets. His sister had also read storybooks to him before he went to sleep. She had crawled under the covers with him and read until he fell asleep.

"Bausch!" shouted a shrill voice. Sasha jumped off his seat. He almost fell at the feet of a tall, thin woman.

"We are here," replied Mama in a calm voice.

"Come," commanded the woman. She turned quickly back into the office behind the doors. Mama gave Sasha's arm a little squeeze. He followed her through the double doors.

It was warmer in the inner office. The tall woman stood behind a huge wooden desk. She studied Sasha and Mama as they entered the room.

"You may hang your coats there," said the woman. She pointed a long finger at a spindly coat rack by the door. Sasha helped Mama out of her coat. Then he took off his gloves. He placed them in his pockets with shaking hands.

"Sit here," ordered the woman. They sat on two stiff chairs. She was reading a thick folder of papers. Then she sat back in her chair. She folded her arms and smiled at Sasha.

Sasha stared into the woman's dark, granite eyes. He suddenly felt very cold again. A shiver crawled up his back. His hope faded.

The woman said, "I am Carina Mikalonova. I have

not met you before, Doctor Bausch. However, it looks as though you have applied to leave Russia many times. Why is that?"

Sasha watched his mother swallow hard and raise her chin. She said in a calm voice, "My husband needed to leave for health reasons. He was granted a visa with my daughter more than two years ago. We wish to join him. My son needs his father. We had heard there were changes in the emigration rules."

Carina Mikalonova's eyes swept over to Sasha. He hoped the woman couldn't see him shiver.

"Do you miss your papa?" she asked. Sasha watched her lips curve up again. Her eyes never smiled.

"Yes, madam," Sasha replied in a whisper.

"Hmm," said the woman. She thumbed through the papers. "There was quite a sum of money in the family before. You were successful capitalists before the revolution." She did not bother to hide her disgust.

"Now it says that you have only your wages from the hospital. How can this be?" She smoothed her dark hair back into its tight knot. Sasha wondered if it made her head hurt to wear her hair so tightly drawn back.

Mama answered, "Those funds are lost to us. The money was invested long before the war. Unfortunately, my husband's family invested in German bonds. They became worthless. Everything else was acquired by the state."

Carina raised an eyebrow.

"Justly so," Mama quickly added. She held her hands apart. "Prices are high. My salary from the hospital barely maintains our small household. I have a small savings . . ."

"How much?" asked Carina. Suddenly, she looked interested.

"I have 30 **rubles** left from the sale of some jewelry," offered Mama hopefully.

Carina flipped her hand, disgusted. "No other jewelry?" she questioned.

Mama shook her head. "All sold."

Carina Mikalonova tapped her fingers against her sharp chin. She smoothed out imaginary wrinkles on her soft wool dress. On her hand, a large ring with glittering stones captured the light.

She said, "I don't see a change in your case, madam. You would not qualify under the new orders. As a medical doctor, you are necessary to the state. You say there is nothing you can offer—no funds that can be . . . found. Then I am afraid there is nothing I can do. Perhaps your husband should return to you."

The woman's lips curved up again. "Or perhaps those investments will soon be worth more." She looked hard at Mama and then stood.

Wordlessly, Sasha and Mama retrieved their coats

and left the office. Mama held her head high. She marched down the steps and out through the iron gate. Sasha jumped when the guard slammed it shut.

Mama rushed through the crowded streets. She said nothing. Silently, Sasha hurried along behind her. He tried to keep up with her pace. She stopped at the river's edge and leaned out over the railing. Staring into the distance, she took several deep breaths.

Mama turned to Sasha. She asked forcefully, "How is it possible to convince someone you are poor?" She shook her head. "I'm sorry, darling. I will find a way. I will. I wish I weren't so valuable to the state! Then they would let us go."

Sasha saw his mother brush a tear from her cheek. "Mama, I am happy here with you and Poppy. Honestly, I don't mind," he lied. He really wanted his family together again.

"Someday it will be different," he said. "I would have missed Albert and Poppy anyway." That was not a lie.

Mama smiled. "Come on, then," she said. "At least you didn't have to do Latin."

7
Spring River

Poppy could tell that things hadn't gone well at the emigration office. She didn't say anything as she ushered Sasha into the kitchen. Warm chicken soup with tiny bits of real chicken bubbled on the coal stove. Poppy dished up a bowl of soup for Sasha.

Sasha slurped the last of the broth from his bowl. He finally felt warm again.

"Now go put on your good clothes. You can hurry down to school," said Poppy.

"Couldn't I stay home just this once, Poppy?" begged Sasha.

"No, Sasha," said Mama. She hurried into the kitchen. She was dressed in her starched hospital uniform. "You will need your schooling. Every day is important—and every subject."

Sasha pretended to pout.

"Even Latin," Mama continued. She waved on her way out.

Sasha awoke late in the night. He heard voices in the kitchen. He had not seen Mama that evening. She had worked late at the hospital. Now Sasha recognized her voice and the other deep, quiet one.

He wrapped himself in a blanket and slipped out of his warm bed. Sasha's feet were unhappy as they landed on the icy floor. His ears drew him forward to the softly lit kitchen.

He stood back a few paces from the kitchen door and listened to the familiar voices.

"I just don't know which way to turn anymore, Lazare," cried Mama softly. "There is no way for Victor to come back. I cannot convince the government that I have nothing. Yet I have nothing to bribe them with. I must do something soon. I feel so trapped."

"Yes, it is a very big trap," chuckled the old man. "But we will be clever mice, eh? We will spring this trap."

"And land yourself back in the gulag or be shipped off to Siberia? I will not see that happen again. This must be my doing alone," Mama insisted.

"But I can advise, can't I? This old man can still do a bit of thinking," said Lazare. "There must be a way. Old people are sometimes worth a bit—even if not to the state."

"Yes," said Mama. Suddenly, she sounded hopeful. "Old people . . . " she repeated. Their voices faded as his mama and old Lazare moved off toward the hall.

Sasha tiptoed back to bed. "Old people can help, and so can young," he whispered to himself. His toes were very glad to be warm again.

He heard the front door close. Just as he settled to sleep, he heard his mother's voice.

"Good night, Sasha."

Sasha and Mama walked by the river near **Red Square**. The sun glistened on the many colored domes of **St. Basil's Cathedral**. Sasha stared up at the towering cathedral.

"I used to imagine the domes had been painted by little children," he said. "I would play a game and choose my favorite one for the day. Would it be the blue and yellow one? No, I think the tall red one is the winner today."

"I love the way they are all different," agreed Mama. "My favorite is always the green one."

Moscow's people spilled out onto the huge square. They came to enjoy the first warmth of spring. They wandered along the riverbanks.

The high walls of the **Kremlin** towered above them. No one skated on the iced river now. Warning flags fluttered in the soft breeze.

In the vendors' stalls, hawkers sold warm rolls shaped like birds. Sasha crunched the sweet bread. He savored the raisins used for eyes.

Sasha scanned the sky to see if he could find one of the returning larks.

"I am glad for the spring," sighed Mama. She lifted her face to the warmth.

Sasha sighed. "Mama, what will we do? About being together again, I mean. Please don't treat me like a child any longer. I need to know what will happen."

Mama looked at Sasha for a long moment. Then she replied, "Yes, Sasha. You are right. You are old enough to understand what is happening."

She stopped and considered for a moment. "The problem is that I don't always know what is to come."

"I know," agreed Sasha. "But sometimes I feel like a leaf blown into the wide river. I flow with the currents and try to keep from sinking. I need to feel like I am in control of my life. I want to help make the decisions. It's my life."

"You are not the only one who feels that way," considered Mama. "I feel like this frozen river. On the surface, I am unable to move. But underneath, I know there are many changes to come—and soon."

"Lazare has told me something of the trouble in Russia. I can read the newspaper. I can see the posters on the walls," insisted Sasha.

"Papers and posters are not where the truth lies, Sasha," warned Mama. "You must understand. I want you away from here soon. If that means that I come later . . ."

"Somehow, we'll find a way," consoled Sasha. "You must let me help. I could quit school to earn some money. I know I could get a job in the market or perhaps . . ."

"No," Mama said quickly. But she smiled.

Sasha confessed, "I want so much to be with Da and Raisa. But how can I leave Poppy and Albert? And now you say I must go alone? I just want us all to be together. I want us to be a family again."

Mama nodded slowly. She hugged him gently and said, "We will always be a family—even if we are sometimes apart."

In the distance, Sasha heard a low rumble echo along the river. He turned to watch a huge crack in the ice. The crack grew wider across the frozen surface. Other cracks appeared. The rumble increased.

People called from the edge in excitement. Others ran so they could see the breakup. The split in the ice widened.

Then the river began to move—slowly at first, then with increasing speed. Ice was propelled into the air. Huge chunks tipped on end as the black water surged from below. Thunder filled the air. The river was alive with the signs of spring.

Sasha grinned at his mother. "We are on the move!" he shouted above the roar.

8
Sudzal

Sasha counted the days until his visit with his grandparents. He and Mama planned to take the train.

Poppy fussed, "This is not a good time to travel. The rivers are high with spring melt. And the roads are a sea of mud."

"Earlier, we could have gone by **troika** down the frozen river," agreed Mama. "But not now that the river is melting.

"But we must go anyway. I do not have much time left to see Poppop and **Babushka**. They are getting old, and the country is changing. Victor would want me to take care of his parents now."

Mama smiled and patted Poppy's arm. "We will be fine, Poppy. Sasha will be a help on the train. It is only a day's trip to Sudzal."

Poppy packed food for the daylong trip. She helped them carry it to the station. They set out walking early.

"Poppy, we will have enough to feed the whole train," Sasha joked. He shifted the heavy cloth bag from one shoulder to the other. Poppy and Mama carried their clothing in two old leather cases.

Mama huffed a bit but did not slacken her pace. "We had better hurry if we want to ride together," she said.

Sasha had to run to keep up. The station echoed. It was almost empty in the early morning. They crossed the huge hall. Mama stopped to see which track held their train. Sasha's nose wrinkled at the smells of burned oil and coal dust.

Poppy helped Sasha and Mama up the steps and onto the train. Others shoved past them, hurrying to find a seat. Sasha and Mama sat near a window in their compartment. Poppy waved at them.

"See you in a week!" shouted Sasha. He waved back.

Mama and Sasha had to share a seat in the last car. Sasha didn't care. He spent most of the day with his nose pressed to the dirty window. He spotted fields of winter wheat that were beginning to turn green. And he saw dirt fields ready for the spring planting.

Small villages crowded the river's edge on a rocky hilltop. Thick forests, dark as night, swallowed the train at times, only to spit it out again onto more sunny open fields. Cowardly snow hid from the sun on north-facing hills and under trees.

They arrived in Sudzal late in the afternoon. Sasha loved the small town. It reminded him of a magic kingdom from an old storybook. Ancient white walls surrounded a beautiful church. The golden spires of the cathedral glowed in the dimming light.

"Do Babushka and Poppop know we are coming today?" asked Sasha. He looked for his grandparents as they climbed down the steps of the train.

"Yes, but I wrote to them to wait at home. It is only a short way," said Mama cheerfully. "And you ate most of the food. So we don't have much to carry."

Narrow logs lined the street through town. They made it easier to walk in the thawing mud. Once out of town, Mama and Sasha followed a muddy gravel road.

The sun shone between the trees of the forest. Clumps of brown snow blanketed the spreading roots of large trees. Green shoots of grass bravely poked through.

"Look, Sasha, a crocus," said Mama. She pointed to the small yellow flower bud peeping through the snow. "It's almost spring."

Sasha noticed something else peeking out. A tiny cottage hunched near the side of the road. A small child stood in the doorway.

Sasha could not tell if the child was a boy or girl. Its clothes hung in rags. Its hair fell limply, covering eyes and shoulders.

The child's face was very thin. Sasha was reminded of Lazare when he had first returned home. The child's swollen belly rested on top of skinny, sticklike legs.

"Mama?" whispered Sasha. He touched her arm.

"Yes, I see, Sasha. Do you have anything left from Poppy's lunch?" she asked quietly.

Sasha searched through the food bag. "Only this one apple and part of a loaf of bread," he replied.

"Give it to her," said Mama.

"It's not much." Sasha looked upset.

"But it may save her," said Mama. She took the food from Sasha.

Mama approached the child. She held out the food in her hands. The child hesitated. But then she responded to Mama's smile.

"Go on. Take it, please," Mama said softly.

Tiny hands accepted the offering. The hungry child closed the door slowly.

"I'm sorry I ate so much on the train," cried Sasha softly. "I didn't know."

"We didn't know, Sasha," comforted Mama. They continued on their way.

Sasha's grandparents' house was at the edge of the village. The tiny home was built of logs. It had a steep tiled roof. There were small windows on the front of the house. They were framed with carved wood that had been painted blue. A wooden fence separated the garden from the street.

Sasha undid the latch to the gate. He called to his grandmother, "Babushka!"

Immediately, Babushka opened the low, rounded wooden door. She gave a great cry and threw up her hands in joy. She was very small and frail. Sasha thought she seemed thinner than the last time he had seen her.

A bright printed scarf covered her wiry gray hair. In

her excitement, her patched blue woolen shawl had fallen from her shoulders.

Sasha dropped the bag he carried. He flew into his grandmother's open arms. She patted him all over, calling his name softly.

Then Mama came up to the door. She was properly hugged and inspected.

"Poppop, look. They have come!" cried the old woman. She pulled them into the house through the low doorway. Sasha didn't remember having to duck last time.

"Look, your grandson is here. And he is taller than I am," Babushka shouted proudly.

"Hello, Poppop," said Sasha. He remembered to speak up because of the old man's deafness. Sasha stood before his grandfather's chair. The old man looked up and grinned toothlessly.

"Sasha!" cried Poppop. "Come here and let me see you."

Sasha bent down and let the old man hug him. Then Mama hugged Poppop as well. They all sat down to talk.

Soon the cottage grew dim as evening approached. Babushka led Sasha and Mama to the small table below the window. In the gloom, a single candle waited to be lit. A round loaf of crusty black bread stood guard beside a small wedge of cheese.

"I have some apples left from our tree. Perhaps Sasha could get them from the cellar. All the potatoes are gone, I'm afraid," apologized Babushka.

Mama glanced at the meager fare. She quickly said to Sasha, "We just ate on the train. Didn't we, Sasha? Poppy packed us a very big meal."

Sasha was puzzled for a moment. Then he caught his mother's signal and agreed. "Oh, yes, Babushka. We could only eat a little. I am so full."

They sat together and watched the old people eat. Sasha's stomach grumbled. He nibbled a small piece of the bitter bread.

Later that evening, Mama came to say good night. Sasha was nestled away in the small bedroom in the attic. His bed was built into the wall above the fireplace. It felt snug and warm against the cold of the cottage room.

"Thank you, Sasha, for understanding about dinner," said Mama.

"What are we going to do about tomorrow?" asked Sasha. "I'm very hungry."

"I know. I have brought some of our savings. You and I will go to town and bring home what we can. I didn't know that life had become so difficult here. I know it is hard for Poppy to find enough food for us in the city. But I had heard things were better in the country."

"But what will they do when we leave?" worried Sasha. "Should they come and live with us?" He was afraid. Sasha remembered how the pawns had been without bread.

Mama smiled. "Sasha, I think that might be a good idea. Don't worry now. I think everything will work out soon. Give me my hug. One for now and one for later," she whispered.

Sasha's stomach grumbled as Mama blew out the candle stub.

Sasha sat with Poppop in the fresh morning air. The sun was strong. It warmed the old log home. Sasha felt good with his back to the wall and his face to the light.

Poppop pick up a half-carved piece of wood. It rested on the rustic bench under the window. Sasha could see flowers and a charging lion emerging from the plank.

The old man pulled a small folding knife from his pocket. He chipped at the wood. Poppop had to move the piece close to his eyes to inspect his work.

"There are some pieces of wood over there in that bin," suggested the old man loudly. He pointed to a wooden box with his knife. "Pick one out and bring it here."

Sasha lazily inspected the odd-shaped hunks in the bin. Finally he chose a piece with a large knot. He rubbed the wood with his hands. The bark was rough. It flaked under the pressure of his fingers. He showed it to Poppop.

"That's good. Now sit here and clean it up just like I showed you last time. Clean off the bark. Get to know the piece of wood. Try to see what shapes will work with it," instructed Poppop.

"Yes, Poppop," said Sasha. He took the small whittling knife his grandfather offered.

They worked in silence for a while. The warmth of the sun blanketed them.

"I heard that Lazare has returned," Poppop finally said.

"Yes, he came to dinner one night. I have played chess with him too," replied Sasha. "He has been very ill. Poppy is always baking him something. She says he will soon be stronger. Mama explained that Lazare said something wrong."

"Not wrong, exactly. He just said it to the wrong people. Lazare always did say what he thought," continued Poppop. "Even as a boy."

"He is still very weak," said Sasha.

"It was a high price to pay," said Poppop. He shook his head. The old man inspected Sasha's efforts with the wood.

"There, that is good, Sasha. You have cleaned your piece well. What do you want to make with it?"

Sasha eyed his chunk from each direction. "I think I would like to try a bear. I could use the change in colors here to show the fur around his neck. Do you think the legs would be too difficult?" asked Sasha. He suddenly felt inspired.

"No, I can show you how to rough them in. Yes, I think that will be a fine piece," agreed Poppop.

Mama called from the door, "Sasha, we will go to town soon. We need to get to the market early. Get your coat. And don't forget to brush your hair."

"Oh," groaned Sasha. He didn't want to leave his work.

Poppop patted him on the knee. "Go on now," he said. "We will have plenty of time later."

Sasha followed his mother down the muddy road back into the small town. Today was market day. Wagons clogged the road. Many people on foot joined them. Some carried baskets with goods they hoped to sell. Others had makeshift packs on their backs.

Mama gave Sasha two empty baskets she hoped to fill. She carried one herself. They entered the town and soon found the market area. Most of the stalls had only a few things displayed. No one seemed to be buying.

Sasha helped Mama find eggs, butter, and several

fresh loaves of bread. They also bought cabbages, potatoes, and some herbs. The prices were high. Soon their money was spent.

Sasha couldn't understand why Mama looked so discouraged. The baskets were heavy in his arms. His stomach rumbled at the thought of dinner.

"I know it's early spring," she said. "So there aren't many vegetables." She looked over the quiet market. "But there is so little to buy here. It is even worse than I suspected."

Sasha's stomach continued to growl. He and Mama headed home, lugging the full baskets.

They passed the small cottage where they had seen the starving child. Mama handed Sasha a loaf of bread, a cabbage, and some potatoes. He carefully placed the food on the step.

"Can we eat soon, Mama?" asked Sasha.

"Yes," laughed Mama. "My tummy is talking too. I'll fix everyone a nice dinner. Then we need to have a family talk."

9

Conversation of Pawns

Mama lit a candle stump. She set it on the table. The wavering light lit the two old faces. Sasha and Mama sat across the table.

"Babushka, Poppop, we need your help," began

Mama. She spoke in a loud voice so that Poppop could hear everything.

"But how can we help?" asked the old man.

"What is it, darling?" said Babushka.

"We want you to come and live with us in Moscow," continued Mama. "Sasha needs his family with him. With Victor gone, we are alone. Raisa's old room has had little use. Please. Won't you come?"

The two old people looked at each other in the candlelight.

"Oh, no—" began Babushka. She shook her head slowly.

"Yes, I think we should," interrupted Poppop. "It's not getting any better here." He looked at Babushka.

"It is only because we are so old that they have left us alone so far. I have been called a **kulak**. So many of our friends have already been sent to Siberia or worse.

"It is only a matter of time before we are driven from this home," Poppop continued. "Just as we were driven from the other. Soon there will be no one left who knows the land."

Turning back to Mama, Poppop said, "But we don't want to burden you, Marie."

"The burden comes with having you so far from us," replied Mama. She put out her hands and covered theirs. "Then it is settled. We can help you can pack. And in a few days, you will return with us."

The old woman looked out over the darkened room. Shifting candlelight wavered across the floor. The shadows of budding tree branches rustled in the wind.

"Yes, I guess it is time," she sighed.

In the morning, Sasha helped his grandparents pack. Babushka tucked two silver tea glasses and her wedding picture among her few clothes. Poppop took his carving tools and his heavy army coat.

"I survived the **Crimean War** in this old thing," he shouted to Sasha. Sasha noticed the medals pinned to the front of the heavy brown coat.

In the quiet evenings, Poppop and Sasha carved by the firelight. Sasha was proud when his bear was finished. It was good for his first try.

On the last day, Sasha's grandparents went to their neighbors. They gave away their remaining possessions. No one had the money to buy them.

Without a backward glance, the old couple closed the rounded wooden door. Together they headed down the muddy road to the train. A kind neighbor followed with their few belongings tied to his mule.

Sasha waited for Albert on the front steps. Albert dashed down the steps. He stuffed his red curls under a knitted cap.

"My mother says I still have to wear this," Albert complained. "Even with the warm weather. Come on. The sledding area will close soon if the weather stays like this."

Under blue skies, the boys set off down the street. Albert pulled a sled behind them. Water trickled as snow quickly melted in the warm air.

"My grandparents came back to Moscow with us," said Sasha.

"Did you have to give up your bed?" asked Albert. "My aunt and uncle came to live with us for a while last year. I had to sleep on the floor."

"No, I guess I'm lucky. We still had Raisa's room," said Sasha. "I'm glad they're here. My Poppop and Lazare have been talking together every night."

"Do you listen?" asked Albert.

"No, I always get caught," said Sasha.

Albert looked disappointed. "How will you know what is going on?" he complained.

Sasha shrugged. "Maybe I don't want to know."

Soon Sasha and Albert arrived at the sled run. They reached the top of the stairs. Puffing, the boys looked out over the open field below them. The remaining snow glistened in the strong light.

The miniature mountain of wood had a steep, iced track. It opened onto a field below. There was plenty of room for a sled to coast to a stop.

Albert lined up the runnerless sled in the icy track. "You can be in front this time, Sasha," he offered.

The boys climbed aboard. They scooted forward. The sled began to gather speed. Sasha was tempted to close his eyes.

They streaked down the icy hill. Sasha couldn't breathe. He felt himself falling. His stomach rose to his throat. The wind rushed past, stinging his eyes. Then they raced out onto the open field and coasted to a gradual stop.

"That was so fast!" yelled Albert. "Race you back to the top."

10
Gambit

"There are more **purges**. Stalin has made arrests for **Kirov's** murder," announced Mama as she burst through the door. "I heard it on the radio at the hospital."

Lazare and Sasha looked up from their chess game.

"Purges? We haven't heard," said Lazare.

"The radio has been broken for a month," complained Poppy. "There's no one to repair it. And I couldn't find replacement tubes anywhere."

"Did Stalin order the purges?" Lazare asked Mama.

Mama nodded solemnly. "It was not said, but that is the rumor."

"Oh dear, now Stalin will make his move. He has been readying himself. It will be worse than last time," sighed Lazare.

The old man moved slowly to the window. He stared out into the darkness. "Oh dear," he repeated to himself.

"What do we do?" Mama asked urgently.

"We must move quickly," urged Lazare. He turned back to face them. "We must hurry the plan along, Marie."

Mama came and sat next to Sasha. "What plan?" asked Sasha.

"Sasha, Lazare has thought of a way to get you to your father," explained Mama. "He thinks it might work."

"Just me?" questioned Sasha. "I told you before. I won't go without you, Mama."

Mama looked into Sasha's face. "I will not be able to go—not now anyway. Lazare thinks you could go with your grandparents. Then we might get you out.

We were going to wait until summer. But now I think we must hurry. I was going to tell you soon, Sasha. But there is no time left."

"Do Poppop and Babushka know?" asked Sasha.

"Yes, I have spoken to them," said Lazare. "They are willing. I can prepare the guardianship papers now. You can sign them tonight, Marie. Then on Monday, Sasha can take them to emigration and try for the visa. There is so little time."

Tears welled in Sasha's eyes. "No! I won't go!" he shouted. "Not without you. No, Mama!" He ran from the room.

"Sasha," called Mama.

"Give him some time. He will see," urged Lazare.

A while later, Lazare opened the door to Sasha's room. Quietly, he sat on the edge of the bed.

Sasha continued to look out the window. Outside, the beech tree's limbs were bursting with new buds. The tree would be green soon.

"I can't go alone, Lazare. I want to be in Riga with everyone. We have been a broken family for too long. I just can't go without Mama!" Sasha whispered.

Lazare took a rattled breath. "Are you a man now, Alexander Victorovich, or a little boy? What your mother does is for your family. Your father and your sister need you, Sasha. They will need your strength as you grow to be a man."

"But Mama. What about her? She will be left behind," cried Sasha.

"Poppy and I will watch over her. Your mother is a strong, capable woman. And there is always hope. There may be another time when she can come. Until then, you have to be the brave one. You have to take control of the situation. You must take your grandparents to safety and be with your father and sister."

"But—" began Sasha.

The old man continued, "It is what your mother wants. No one can do this unless you take control."

Sasha stared out the window. Lazare left quietly.

Later, Sasha reappeared in the parlor. Poppop and Babushka huddled close to the fire. Mama stared out the window. She watched the rain pounding the street below. Lazare worked quietly at the table.

"I'll go, Mama. If it's what you really want," blurted Sasha. He knew if he didn't say it quickly, he would never get it out.

"Yes, Sasha. It is what I want for you," said Mama. But she did not smile.

Lazare nodded to Sasha. "This must not be talked about yet, Sasha. No one, not even Albert, can know of the plan. Do you understand?"

Sasha nodded as Mama enveloped him in her arms. "One for now and one for later."

11

Check

The following evening, Mama said, "Lazare needs to see you, Sasha. Please go and visit him for a moment."

"Yes, Mama," replied Sasha. He closed the door to

his own apartment. Quietly, he made his way down the dark, damp hall to his neighbor. His knock was answered quickly.

"Sasha, tomorrow you must take Babushka and Poppop to emigration by yourself," said Lazare. He closed the door behind Sasha. Sasha groaned inwardly.

"Here are the legal papers. They will prove that your grandparents are your guardians," the old man explained. "We have filled out all the applications for the visa again. You are to ask for Major Kraskoff. Do not mention your mother's name or mine. If anyone asks, your mother has been ill. Your father's family has been taking care of you."

"It is hard for me to lie, Lazare. My ears always get red. Then I start to stammer," said Sasha.

"It's not exactly a lie, Sasha," suggested Lazare. "Babushka has been helping to care for you since Poppy caught that cold."

Sasha looked doubtful, but nodded. "Major Kraskoff?"

Lazare held a small leather pouch out for Sasha. "This is what you must place on top of the papers when you see Major Kraskoff. Make sure there are no other officials in the room when you do," instructed Lazare.

Lazare placed the pouch in Sasha's hand. It

weighed more than Sasha expected. He could feel a few round coins slipping around inside. Sasha carefully untied the pouch. Three gold coins rolled into his hand.

Sasha took a quick breath.

"Keep it safe. It is all there is," said Lazare.

Sasha nodded slowly. He stared at the shiny coins.

"Where did you get them?" he questioned. Then he noticed the empty chessboard by the old man's chair.

"You will be fine," Lazare reassured him quickly. He did not want to explain. "Poppy will help you get your grandparents to the gate. Then you can manage the rest."

Sasha turned to leave. Then he forced himself to ask the difficult question. "Lazare, will you and Mama be in trouble if we do this?"

Lazare looked at him seriously. He replied, "It is a chance we are willing to take, Sasha."

The guard let them through the gate at noon. It was Poppy's idea to arrive late. They waited in the line a long time. Hopefully, the guard would not recognize Sasha from the earlier visit. Sasha wore a different hat and an old coat borrowed from Lazare.

The hallway was stuffy and crowded. "We wish to

see Major Kraskoff," Sasha told the guard. He hoped his voice wouldn't break. The guard grunted and pointed up the stairs.

Sasha hustled his grandparents past the first set of doors. They climbed the steep steps. Sasha was relieved that they had not seen the thin woman again. All of them waited outside Major Kraskoff's office.

Then they were called. Sasha placed the papers on the major's desk. He added the small pouch that Lazare had given to him. The major eyed Sasha and the old people. They stood silently before his desk.

The major leaned back in his chair. He stroked his bushy mustache. "Why do you wish to leave your country?" he asked.

Sasha kept his eyes down. He answered the question in a strong voice.

"My grandparents are old. They are nothing but a burden to the state. My father, who lives in Latvia, has asked me to bring them to him. I—I will then return to my mother. She has been ill." Sasha hoped his ears were not too red.

The major picked up the pouch. He weighed it carefully in his hand.

With a nod, he stamped their visas. Then he quickly pocketed the bribe.

"You will have to wait two days before the visa is valid," said the major. "You must travel in the two days after that. Then . . ." The major shrugged his shoulders.

"Yes, sir. Thank you, sir," said Sasha. He grabbed the official papers from the major. Sasha quickly ushered his grandparents out the door.

"And don't smile as you leave," ordered the major.

Sasha hurried his grandparents down the stairs as fast as he could. He feared the major would change his mind. They reached the first floor. Sasha looked up to see Carina Mikalonova standing at the door of her office.

Sasha quickly pulled his billed cap down over his eyes. He tried to hide behind his grandfather.

They hurried silently past her. Sasha stared at the floor. He could feel her cold eyes follow him down the hall. They passed the guard.

It was all Sasha could do not to pick up Babushka and carry her down the steps. His feet moved in slow motion. It felt like a bad dream.

Finally, they walked through the gate. Sasha took a deep breath. He carefully looked over his shoulder. Carina Mikalonova watched them from the top step.

"Perhaps she didn't know me," he mumbled to himself. They crossed the street and blended into the afternoon crowd. Somehow, though, Sasha knew that she had.

RIVER OF ICE

Albert sat with Sasha in the small square facing their apartment building. The breeze waved gently. The lilac trees in the square dripped lavender, white, and purple onto the new green grass. A thick sweetness hung in the air. Newly awakened bees hummed in the trees.

Albert chattered happily. "I am going to visit my aunt and uncle this summer. My mother says that you can come with me. We will have to help with chores in the morning. But there's a good stream for fishing and loads of mushrooms. I can't wait to go. My mother says that she will ask Poppy to take us on the train and—"

Sasha looked at him miserably.

"What's the matter, Sasha? You always said you wanted to go with me to my uncle's **dacha**. We are finally old enough," continued Albert.

"I—I don't think I can go this summer," stammered Sasha.

"But why?" cried Albert.

"I can't say," sighed Sasha. He hesitated. "I—I might have to go to school." Lying made his ears burn.

"You don't have to go to school." Albert eyed him suspiciously. "What is it? I know you're not telling me. See, your ears look like radishes. You can't tell your best friend?" cajoled Albert.

Sasha sighed. "I'm not supposed to tell you until Friday. I'm not supposed to tell anybody."

"What's special about Friday?" asked Albert. He was getting angry. "Some friend," he muttered and stood up. He glared down at Sasha with arms crossed.

"I'm going on a trip . . . with my grandparents," whispered Sasha, giving in. "Please, please don't say anything. I could get in terrible trouble. You have to promise me, Albert."

"I won't tell anyone," Albert assured him. "Where are you going?"

"Latvia," whispered Sasha.

Albert sat down in silence. They stared out over the blooming square. "You're not coming back. Are you?" he asked quietly.

Sasha only shook his head. For a long while, they sat in silence. The only sound was the buzzing of bees.

"I'll miss you," said Albert solemnly.

They stood and kissed each other on the cheek three times.

"Good-bye," said Sasha. He turned and walked home slowly.

"Das-ve-dahn-ya," said Albert.

Sasha sat in his room staring at the empty suitcase. Poppy had said to choose the things he would need most in Latvia.

He said out loud to himself, "How do I know what I will need? I have never been to Latvia. How can I fit my life into one small leather case?"

Sasha stared at the bag. He was leaving behind all the friends he had in the world—Albert, Lazare, Poppy, Mama.

Mama knocked and entered his room. Sasha quickly brushed away the tear that had fallen. Mama came and sat beside him.

"It's not easy to decide what to keep and what to leave behind," she said. She looked at the empty case. "Perhaps you should take the things that will remind you of the people who love you. Here, I brought your book of Russian fairy tales. I know you are too old for the stories. But it might remind you of reading with me by the fire."

Sasha took the book from her hand. He stared at the old red leather binding. He traced the raised gold lettering.

He thought for a moment. Then he said, "I think I'll take my marbles, the bear I carved with Poppop, and the woolen hat that Poppy knitted for my birthday."

"Good," said Mama.

"You will come as soon as you can?" asked Sasha.

"As soon as I can, Sasha. I promise we will be together again," she whispered.

Sasha knew Mama kept her promises.

It was his last day. Poppy had fixed his favorite lunch—**piroshki**. Sasha could not even taste the puffy pastry filled with meat. Lazare stared at the untouched food on his plate. Poppy sniffled behind her handkerchief.

Mama poured another glass of strong tea from the samovar. She suggested, "Sasha, perhaps you should go and tell Albert that you are going."

"I . . . I already told him," confessed Sasha. "I told him yesterday. But I made him promise not to tell."

Mama frowned but said nothing.

Lazare smiled at Sasha. "We must trust someone. Right, Sasha?" Lazare rose slowly from the table. "It is time."

"I'll get my coat," Sasha said. Dragging his feet, he went to his room. He took one last look around. He tried to memorize the hall, his window, and the light in the kitchen.

Poppy stood at the end of the hall with her arms crossed. Sasha ran to her.

She hugged him to her, saying, "I can't go to the

station. I'd just cry the whole time. Here. I want you to take this."

She undid the clasp of her St. Nicholas medallion from around her neck. "St. Nicholas is the patron saint of children and travelers. He will watch over you when I can't."

"I love you, Poppy," Sasha whispered into her ear.

She smiled at him and said, "I'll take good care of your mother."

"I know you will," replied Sasha.

Lazare stood by the front door without his cane. He gave Sasha three kisses on the cheeks and a long hug.

"Say 'hello' to your father for me. It is good that we have had this time together." His blue eyes twinkled.

Sasha clasped the old man's hand, saying, "Good-bye, sir. Thank you." The last words caught in his throat. He couldn't look up.

Mama and Sasha helped his grandparents down the steps. They climbed into a hired carriage. Sasha peeked out of the buggy's dusty window. The old horse pulled the coach slowly away from the curb.

Albert stood on the steps. Sasha waved good-bye to his best friend.

12
Good-Byes

Albert sat on the sunny steps. There was no smile on his face now. He tried not to think of Sasha boarding a train to leave Moscow.

He hadn't been able to say anything when Sasha left in the carriage with his family. He'd barely managed to return Sasha's good-bye wave. Without his best friend, Albert felt alone in the world.

A sleek black car turned onto their street. Albert could hear the rumble of its engine as it approached. He watched with interest.

There were only a few cars in Moscow. High government officials rode in them. He had never seen one on their quiet street before. Then it stopped in front of his building.

The driver let a tall, well-dressed woman out of the backseat. The stranger surveyed the apartment building. She approached the steps where Albert perched.

"Is this where Madame Doctor Bausch lives?" she asked.

Albert stared at the fox fur coat draped over the thin woman's arms. The little fox heads with bright glass eyes gripped their tails in their teeth.

"Boy! Did you hear me? Does Doctor Bausch live here?" she repeated insistently.

Albert jumped up and took a step back. "Yes," he replied tentatively. "Are you sick? She is not here."

"Where is she?" questioned the woman. She adjusted the foxtails over her shoulders.

"Uh . . . I don't know," lied Albert. He took another step back. He felt the wall behind him.

The woman mounted the steps impatiently. She

grabbed Albert roughly by the arm. "Where is Doctor Bausch?"

"I don't know," cried Albert in a panic.

The woman let go of Albert's arm. She smiled at him. Her voice softened.

"I'm sorry," she soothed. "I am a friend. My name is Carina. The doctor is not at the hospital. I have already been there. Has she gone somewhere with her son?"

Albert looked away from the cold eyes, but not soon enough.

"Have they already gone then?" Carina cooed in a silky voice. "I wanted to say good-bye."

"Sasha is going away," confided Albert. "But we are not supposed to say. I didn't want him to go."

"Of course you didn't," consoled Carina. She patted him on the shoulder. "I don't want him to go either."

"Perhaps you could still go and wave good-bye. They just left a little while ago for the train station. You have your fast car," suggested Albert, trying to help.

The woman's lips curved upwards. "Yes," she said. She hurried back to the car.

13
Checkmate

Sasha helped Babushka out of the carriage. They climbed the wide station steps. Mama followed. Poppop insisted on carrying his own bag.

"I can do it!" he shouted over the clamor of the crowd.

Mama purchased their tickets. Then she led them down the long ramp to the awaiting train. The metallic odor of the train station enveloped Sasha. Coal dust choked his throat.

Crowds of people huddled on the platform. Others called through the train's open doors and windows. Bright words were painted on the train. They shouted the virtues of the government.

People were already boarding the train. Travelers pushed bulky cases through open windows or up the steep metal stairs. Mama and Sasha helped the grandparents find seats in their compartment. Then she gave each of them a long hug.

"Good-bye doesn't seem enough to say," she sighed. Babushka patted Mama gently.

"Come with me to the door, Sasha," Mama said quietly.

Sasha followed her out onto the platform again. She turned to him and smiled.

"I know you will be fine," she said. She brushed her fingers gently through his hair. "Until I can come, give a kiss to your father and Raisa for me."

Sasha nodded. His eyes stung. Mama hugged him hard. "One for now and one for later," she whispered.

Sasha looked up over Mama's shoulder. He gave a short gasp. A chill grabbed him. The woman he remembered from the emigration office was there.

Carina Mikalonova stood at the end of the platform.

From her place at the top of the stairs, Carina searched the crowd. She had not seen them yet. Sasha knew she was there for him. Mama followed Sasha's gaze and understood.

"Go, Sasha, now! Hide in the train. Don't show yourself until the train has left the station!" cried Mama. She gave him one quick squeeze. Then she pushed him onto the stairs.

Sasha raced down the narrow hall of the train. He dashed through the compartment door. Sasha dove down between the seats. He began to rummage through their baggage.

"I think I uh . . . I forgot something," he said to Babushka. He hid his head down out of sight. He crawled farther under the seats.

"No, I think it is here. Just a moment," he called.

Sasha hoped that Babushka's long bright skirt hid him from view. Poppop watched him, puzzled. Sasha didn't want to frighten his grandparents. There was no time to explain. His heart thumped loudly, trying to escape from his chest. He waited.

The engineer whistled a warning. Sasha held his breath. The train jolted. Slowly, the big steel wheels gripped and turned. The train inched away from the shadowy station toward the late afternoon light.

As the train began to pull forward, Sasha carefully

crept up to the window. He peered out of the corner through a jagged crack. He kept his face hidden. Sasha watched as Carina approached Mama through the crowd.

Mama made no move to avoid Carina. She waited with her head held high. They stood almost in front of him. He turned his ear to the crack. Sasha could hear their words above the noise.

"Why have you come to the train station?" demanded Carina.

Mama looked her in the eye and replied, "To see off an old friend."

"Where is the boy?" Carina shouted. She grabbed Mama by the arms. The train whistle echoed through the station.

Mama smiled. She replied slowly as the train moved away, "Where he should be."

GLOSSARY

Alexander Victorovich Bausch people in Russia are given a first, second, and last name. The second name is their father's first name with an ending. *Ovich* means "son of" (Alexander Victorovich). *Onova* means "daughter of" (Madame Lazaronova).

Babushka grandmother

blini thin pancakes served with sour cream and fruit preserves

borscht beet and red cabbage soup; served hot or cold

chai a hot Russian tea

czar the title for the ruler of Russia until the 1917 revolution

Crimean War one of the long series of Russian/Turkish wars

dacha a Russian country cottage

gulag the prison system in Russia consisting of labor camps

kasha porridge

GLOSSARY

Kirov, Sergei M. a high Soviet official whose assassination in 1934 was used by Stalin to launch the Great Purges of his political rivals

kopeck a Russian coin (100 kopecks = 1 ruble)

Kremlin a fortress in central Moscow. It was built in 1156 and enlarged several times between the 14th and 16th centuries. It contains 20 towers, many palaces, an armory, and the Cathedral of the Archangel.

kulak any Russian farmer who had other people working for him. Kulaks were killed or forced from their homes during the agricultural upheavals after the revolution.

Lenin, Vladimir Ilich the leader of the Bolsheviks and founder of the Communist Party. He led the revolution in October of 1917 and was dictator of the Soviet Union until his death in 1924.

pirog a fruit tart

piroshki a fried or baked pastry with meat or vegetables inside

GLOSSARY

purges when the Russian government, led by Joseph Stalin, sought to rid itself of political enemies through imprisonment, execution, and deportation

Red Square a huge landmark in the center of Moscow that holds the Kremlin, Lenin's Tomb, and St. Basil's Cathedral

ruble the basic unit of money in Russia

Russian Revolution between 1917 and 1920 when the Bolsheviks controlled Russia. For many centuries, a czar had ruled Russia. Most of the people of the country were very poor. In the early 20th century, there were many small uprisings as various leaders struggled to take control of the country. In 1917, Lenin and a group of men called the Bolsheviks took control of Russia. The czar and his family were exiled and later killed. Between 1918 and 1920, there was a civil war that left the country in ruins. The Bolsheviks maintained control.

St. Basil's Cathedral a famous church in Moscow with colorful onion-shaped domes

samovar a vessel, usually metal, used to heat water for tea. A cylinder in the middle holds burning coal. A small teapot sits on the top of the samovar to hold a strong brew.

Siberia a region in Russia where political prisoners were sent as punishment

Stalin, Joseph the Communist leader who came to power after the death of Lenin. This powerful dictator ruled the Soviet Union from 1929 until 1953. He is believed to be responsible for the deaths of millions of Russians through purges and starvation.

troika a small sled pulled by three horses

visa official permission to visit another country